W9-BKG-005

Tales from India

For Jessica, celebrating only an eighth of your heritage,
but which I hope will give you a lifetime of inspiration. J. G.

To Clare—for your creative spirit and friendship. A. H.

First U.S. edition 2011

Library of Congress Cataloging-in-Publication Data

Gavin, Jamila.
Tales from India / Jamila Gavin ; illustrated by Amanda Hall. —1st U.S. ed.
p. cm.
ISBN 978-0-7636-5564-8
1. Hindu mythology—Juvenile literature. I. Hall, Amanda. II. Title.
BL1216.G35 2011
398.220954—dc22 2010047651

11 12 13 14 15 16 GBL 10 9 8 7 6 5 4 3 2 1

Printed in Shenzhen, Guangdong, China

This book was typeset in Bembo Educational.
The illustrations were done in gouache.

Edited by Emma Goldhawk
Designed by janie louise hunt

TEMPLAR BOOKS

an imprint of Candlewick Press
99 Dover Street
Somerville, Massachusetts 02144
www.candlewick.com

Tales from India

Stories of Creation and the Cosmos

WRITTEN BY JAMILA GAVIN

ILLUSTRATED BY AMANDA HALL

Contents

Introduction

India is a land of travelers, pilgrims, explorers, and merchants who, since the beginning of time, have moved from place to place, taking their stories with them.

As a child growing up in India, I was fascinated by the sight of people taking journeys; solitary figures crossing a vast landscape carrying only a pot and a bundle, with no starting point or destination in sight.

To me, every one of those mysterious journeys had religious meaning. The whole of India—its geography, history, philosophy—is defined by its oldest religion, Hinduism, a religion so ancient that no one is quite sure how long ago it came into being. Hinduism was certainly there long before the written word—a time when stories were passed on by word of mouth. Even now, storytelling is the thread that holds this vast subcontinent together.

To hear or read these stories is to gain a glimmer of understanding of this ancient time. The sea of milk being churned into butter at the start of creation helps us to appreciate why the cow is a holy creature to Hindus.

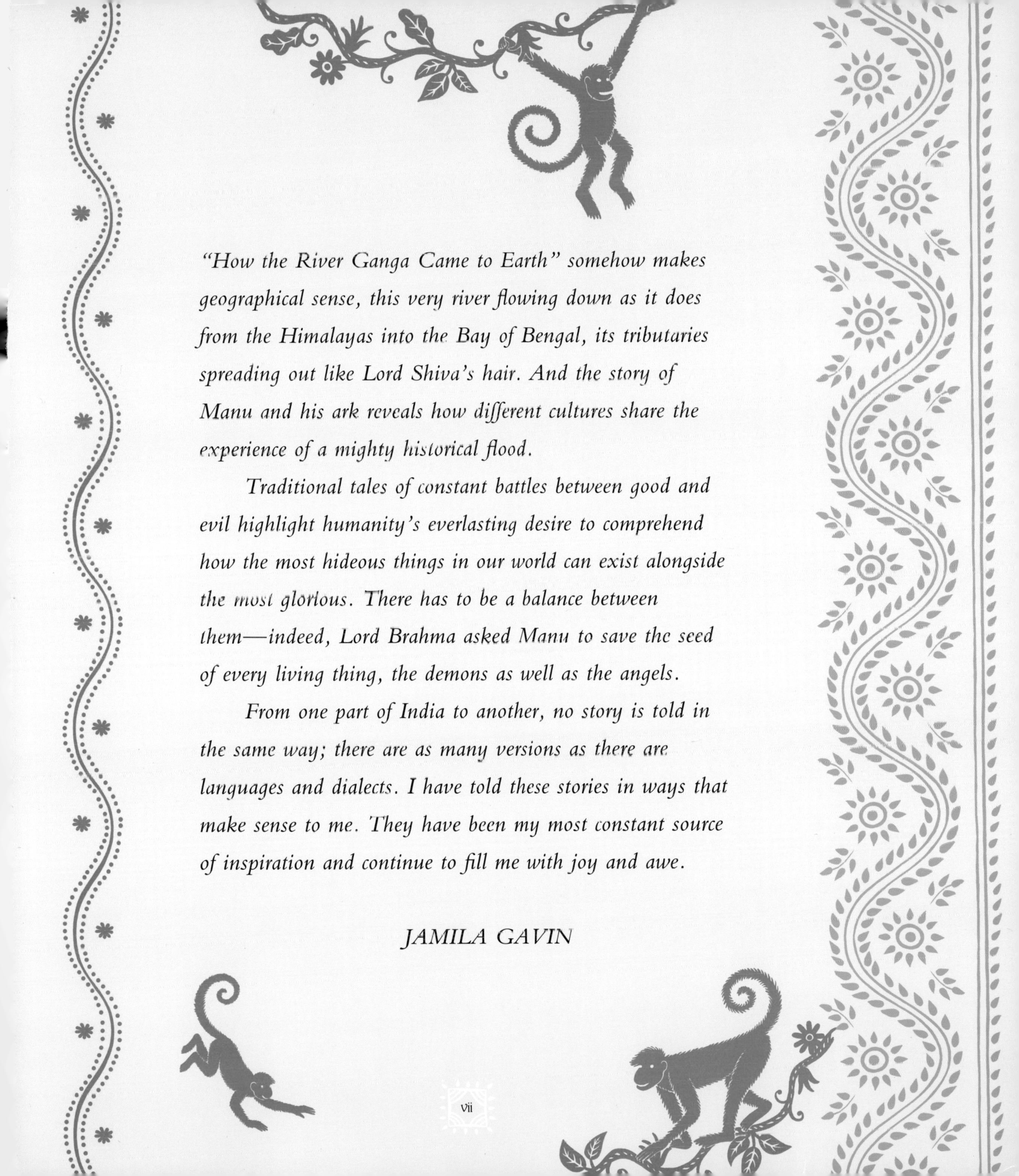

"How the River Ganga Came to Earth" somehow makes geographical sense, this very river flowing down as it does from the Himalayas into the Bay of Bengal, its tributaries spreading out like Lord Shiva's hair. And the story of Manu and his ark reveals how different cultures share the experience of a mighty historical flood.

Traditional tales of constant battles between good and evil highlight humanity's everlasting desire to comprehend how the most hideous things in our world can exist alongside the most glorious. There has to be a balance between them—indeed, Lord Brahma asked Manu to save the seed of every living thing, the demons as well as the angels.

From one part of India to another, no story is told in the same way; there are as many versions as there are languages and dialects. I have told these stories in ways that make sense to me. They have been my most constant source of inspiration and continue to fill me with joy and awe.

JAMILA GAVIN

How the World Began

Before the world began, there was only a white sea of milk. Floating on the sea of milk was a single lotus flower, and sleeping within the flower's pale-pink petals was the Creator, Lord Brahma.

While Lord Brahma slept, there was Nothing. No Earth and sky, no light or darkness, no good or bad, no man or beast. The universe didn't exist at all. There was nothing except the still, silent, milky sea. Life could only begin when Lord Brahma awoke.

Ten thousand years went by; an eternity went by, when suddenly the calm surface of the milky ocean began to quiver. Lord Brahma had opened his eyes.

He looked around him and saw Nothing. How empty everything was; how lonely he felt. Great tears welled up in his eyes. They rolled down his cheeks and fell into the sea of milk and became the Earth. Others he brushed away, and they became the Air and Sky.

Lord Brahma became three in one and one in three: he was Lord Brahma, the Creator; Lord Vishnu, the Preserver; and Lord Shiva, the Destroyer.

Then he stood up and stretched and stretched until his body became the Universe. He stretched to the right and created Day and Night; he stretched to the left and created the Sun, the Moon, and all the stars in the firmament. He stretched this way and that, creating the dry seasons and stormy seasons, Fire, Wind, and Rain. And then he created the gods.

First he created the Devas, the gods of light. They shone with beauty and goodness, and their friends were angels, saints, fairies, and nymphs.

Then he created the Asuras, the gods of darkness. Their friends were goblins, giants, and serpents.

And so he created both friends and enemies, for the Devas and the Asuras were born to be enemies.

Within the sea of milk was a miraculous substance called Amrit. Anyone who drank it would stay young forever. Both the Devas and the Asuras wanted the Amrit, but they could get it only by churning the sea and turning it to butter. But where would they find a churn that was powerful enough for the task?

The Devas and Asuras looked at each other. Even though they were enemies, they would have to work together to get to the Amrit.

The Devas searched in one direction and came to a mountain named Mandara, which was thrusting out of the ocean. "This will make a good churning rod!" they cried.

The Asuras searched in another direction and came across Vasuki, a long and mighty serpent with a hooded head and darting tongue. "He can be our churning rope!" they shouted.

They wound the mighty serpent around and around the mountain, turning it into a churn. The Asuras held the serpent's head, the Devas his lashing tail, and between them, they tugged his body to and fro, back and forth, this way and that, faster and faster. And as the mountain churned the sea, it began to froth and foam. Steam poured from the serpent's mouth.

Lightning flashed, thunder bellowed, and fire and rain swirled about. And still they churned and churned, turning the sea of milk into one vast whirlpool, until at last it began to thicken and set into butter.

The Devas and Asuras fell back, exhausted. The Amrit glistened like dew on the surface of the butter. "It's ours!" cried the Devas.

An angel carrying a goblet appeared and scooped up the precious Amrit.

"No! It's ours!" protested the Asuras.

The two sides began to fight bitterly. Then a demon snatched the goblet from the angel, opened his mouth, and drank the Amrit.

When the Sun and the Moon saw what had happened, they rushed to the rescue. "Stop him!" they cried. "The demon Rahu has swallowed the Amrit. Now the Asuras and their friends the demons will rule the world!"

Lord Brahma heard their cries. He didn't want the Asuras to have all the power, either, so just as the magic liquid was trickling down Rahu's throat, he swiped off his head.

The demon's body plunged to Earth dead, but because the magic liquid was still in his throat, his head soared up into the sky, roaring and bellowing. It would live there forever. His gaping mouth would chase the Sun and the Moon around the heavens, and sometimes he would swallow one and plunge the Earth into darkness. But they would always slip out of Rahu's neck, and light would return.

And so the world was created; the battle had begun between good and evil, light and darkness, Devas and Asuras. And so it would go on and on until Lord Brahma became tired and closed his eyes once more. Then the Universe would cease to exist except for a sea of milk, a lotus flower, and the Lord of Creation, fast asleep.

How Lord Shiva Became Blue-Throated

In the Beginning, when the sea of milk was being churned by the Devas, the gods of light, and the Asuras, the gods of darkness, wonderful things rose from the churning.

From out of the fire and swirling mists appeared a marvelous cow—the provider of Plenty. Then came the Tree of Paradise, whose glorious scent perfumed the world, followed by a magnificent white elephant that Indra, Lord of Heaven, took as his mount, and a mighty white horse for Lord Vishnu, the Preserver.

But everyone was waiting for the most perfect creation of all—the goddess Lakshmi. Lord Vishnu already knew he loved her and that he wanted her to be his queen. Together they would bring happiness, good fortune, and love to the world.

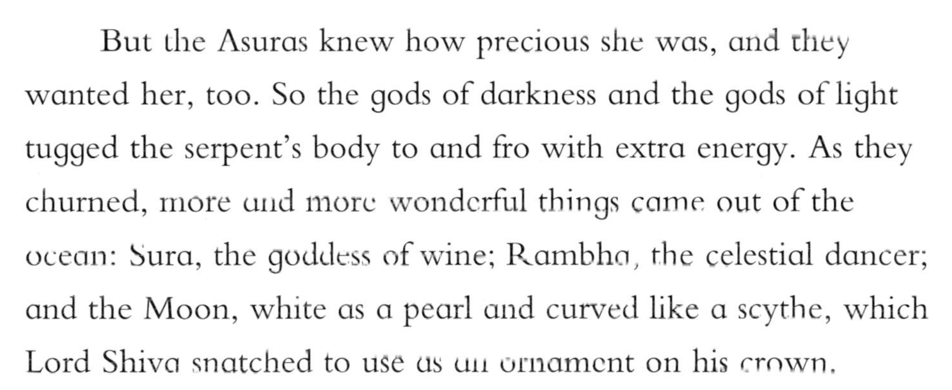

But the Asuras knew how precious she was, and they wanted her, too. So the gods of darkness and the gods of light tugged the serpent's body to and fro with extra energy. As they churned, more and more wonderful things came out of the ocean: Sura, the goddess of wine; Rambha, the celestial dancer; and the Moon, white as a pearl and curved like a scythe, which Lord Shiva snatched to use as an ornament on his crown.

But where was Lakshmi?

Down at the bottom of the sea of milk, where Vishnu, in the shape of a giant turtle, had been carrying the mountain on his back, the churning suddenly ceased; there was a strange trembling, shimmering . . . and Vishnu knew that his beloved Lakshmi, the most perfect of creations, was rising up through the waves.

"You shall be my queen!" exclaimed Lord Vishnu joyfully.

"No!" cried the Asuras. "She's ours!" But they had to resume the churning or Lakshmi would be lost. Angrily, they pulled and twisted the mountain to and fro with the serpent's body, pulling so violently that the creature howled in agony. His torment was so terrible that he opened his mouth and a torrent of venomous blue liquid poured forth.

Also watching was Lord Shiva, the Destroyer, and when he is

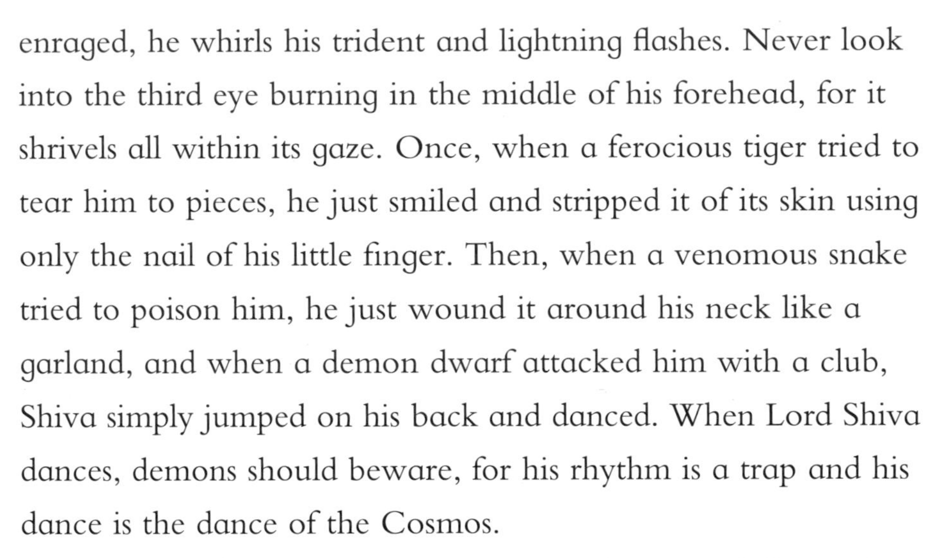

enraged, he whirls his trident and lightning flashes. Never look into the third eye burning in the middle of his forehead, for it shrivels all within its gaze. Once, when a ferocious tiger tried to tear him to pieces, he just smiled and stripped it of its skin using only the nail of his little finger. Then, when a venomous snake tried to poison him, he just wound it around his neck like a garland, and when a demon dwarf attacked him with a club, Shiva simply jumped on his back and danced. When Lord Shiva dances, demons should beware, for his rhythm is a trap and his dance is the dance of the Cosmos.

Shiva couldn't allow the goddess Lakshmi to fall into the hands of the Asuras. With his trident whirling, he came hurtling into the fray. The Asuras shrieked. They would fight to the death. The torrent of poisonous liquid streaming from the serpent's jaws threatened to destroy Lakshmi and the world that Lord Brahma had just created.

In a flash, Lord Shiva leaped forward openmouthed, and the river of poison poured into his mouth. How the fiery blue liquid burned his throat! But Shiva just threw back his head, shook his snaky locks of hair, and shouted, "I am Nilkanth—the Blue-Throated One!"

And so the world was saved.

Joyfully, the goddess Lakshmi sat on Vishnu's knee and became his queen.

Manu, the Fish, and the Flood

Manu, the first man on Earth, stood praying in a stream of cool water.

For many years, he had been standing on one leg with his arms outstretched to Heaven. And, no matter if the sun burned like a furnace, or rains lashed like whips, or fierce animals growled in the jungle, nothing—or so it seemed—could distract him from his pious meditation.

But one day, while Manu was deep in prayer, a tiny horned fish desperately nudged his ankle. "Manu! Help me, help me! There's a big fish trying to eat me up!" Even though Manu's mind was considering the Meaning of Life and the Cause of Everything, he took pity on the little creature and scooped him into his water pitcher. Then he resumed his prayers.

The little fish began to grow, and soon it was too big for the water pitcher. "Manu, Manu! Help me!" it cried. "The water pitcher isn't big enough, and I'm very squashed."

So Manu took the fish and tipped it into a nearby water tank. But the fish continued to grow, and once again it disturbed Manu's prayers. "Manu, Manu! Help me! The water tank isn't big enough, and I can't even flick my tail!"

Manu caught up the fish in his arms and took it to a vast river that ran nearby. This broad, deeply flowing river quenched the thirst of the whole land. "Be happy in this divine river," cried Manu, as he tipped the fish into the holy waters.

But before Manu could resume his prayers, the fish was already calling out, "Manu, Manu! The river's too small, and I've grown so big. I'm caught between the riverbanks, and I can hardly breathe! Take me to the ocean, or I'll die!"

Manu was amazed to see that this was true. Praying to Lord Brahma for strength, Manu heaved the giant fish out of the river and staggered all the way to the ocean. Wading into the waves, he released the fish. With a wriggle of joy, it sped away. But before Manu returned to the shore, the fish reared up out of the sea and called to him.

"Thank you, Manu! Thank you for saving my life. Now listen to what I have to say. Lord Brahma, the Creator, is not very happy with the world. There is too much evil in it, and he wants to destroy everything and start again. But if you do exactly as I say, you will be saved."

Manu listened.

"Go and build an ark," began the fish. "Collect the seed of every living thing to be found in the world and store it on this vessel."

Manu obeyed. He went to the jungles and the deserts, the icy regions and the waterlands, to the vast skies above and to the depths of the ocean, and he collected the seed of every flying, hopping, wriggling, padding, swimming, growling creature that he

could find. He collected the seeds of the Devas and the Asuras, and those of the Seven Holy Scholars, who deliver the words of ancient wisdom. All, whether good or bad, were living things, and all went onto the giant boat.

Then Manu waited for the destruction to begin.

First, seven blazing suns appeared in the sky and were so fiery and hot that soon all the streams, rivers, and oceans dried up. The trees shriveled, the crops failed, and the earth became as hard as iron. Manu was sure that he and all the other creatures would be burned to death as tongues of fire greedily licked their way around the world. So why had he been told to build a boat?

One day, at last, a single black cloud appeared in the sky, followed by another and another. Like a herd of elephants, they rolled across the sky, blotting out the seven suns, and the world was plunged into darkness. Suddenly there was a mighty crack of thunder, and down came the rain.

It rained and rained for twelve years. The streams and rivers and lakes filled up and overflowed and flooded

the land, drowning everything. All that was left was Manu and his boat and all the seeds of every living thing.

When at last the rain stopped, Manu found himself floating on a vast ocean. There was not one speck of life or land on the horizon. How lonely he felt.

Then one day, after many more years, he saw something sticking up out of the waves, something that was swimming rapidly toward him. As Manu looked closely, he could make out the shape of a horn. Desperately, Manu rushed to find a coil of rope, and, making a lasso, he spun it over the side of the boat, caught the horn, and pulled it tight.

The creature leaped and jerked, but Manu wouldn't let go. Even when it turned around and began to swim away, Manu held on for all his worth and found himself and the boat being hauled along behind the creature at great speed.

Year after year, Manu and his ark were dragged across the never-ending waters until, one day, his eyes almost dim from watching and staring and seeing nothing but sea and sky, he glimpsed the tip of a mountain rising up out of the ocean.

With joy he realized that he was being taken toward the mountain. When he heard the bottom of the boat scrape the shale, Manu stumbled ashore and fell, weeping with gratitude, upon dry land.

The creature rose out of the waves. It was the giant

horned fish. Before it swam away, the fish spoke to Manu in a loud and solemn voice. "I am Brahma, Lord of all Living Things, Creator of the Universe. Because you saved my life when I was a little fish in trouble, I have now saved yours. When the waters drop, go and place the seed of every living thing in its proper place so that life can begin all over again."

So Manu went all over the world returning the seeds: back to the deserts, jungles, waterlands, and icy regions; back to the mountains, valleys, oceans, and skies. He returned the stripy, spotted, furry, scaly, winged, and clawed creatures; the stinging,

scratching, slithering, swimming, scampering, and climbing things; as well as the demons who came from the bowels of the Earth and the angels who lived in the highest heavens. Once again, the Seven Holy Scholars began to reveal the ancient words of wisdom that came from the gods.

Every living thing that Lord Brahma had created, Manu returned to its proper place.

His work completed, Manu found himself a cool stream, where he stood on one leg, raised his hands in prayer, and thanked Brahma for creating the Universe all over again.

How the River Ganga Came to Earth

When creation was still new,
the goddess Ganga, a sacred river,
flowed only in Heaven, pouring from
the big toe of Lord Vishnu in the celestial
regions of the Himalayas.

The gods bathed in her holy waters, which cleansed them of their sins and gave them everlasting life.

Down on Earth lived a king called Sagara, who was great and powerful. But although he had two wives, he had no sons to succeed him. So he prayed and meditated and lived a life of such austerity and devotion that, at last, the gods rewarded him. One wife gave birth to one son, but the other wife gave birth to sixty thousand sons.

Having so many sons made King Sagara feel even more powerful—so much so, that he

decided that he wanted to establish his authority beyond any doubt by performing a horse ritual.

A beautiful white horse was to be set free to wander at will over the face of the Earth, asserting the king's sovereignty, before being sacrificed to the gods. A mighty chariot fighter was ordered to follow and protect the horse. But even though it had such fierce protection, one night Indra, Lord of Heaven, who felt threatened by King Sagara's power, secretly stole the horse away and took it to Kapila the Sage for safekeeping.

King Sagara was outraged and sent forth his sixty thousand and one sons to look for it. They encircled the entire Earth and trawled the ocean league by league. When they found no trace of the white horse anywhere on the Earth's surface, they began to burrow down to the Underworld. They dug deep and hard, with hands like thunderbolts and fingers like plowshares, going to all four corners of the world below. They ruthlessly killed anything that got in their way, and frightened voices cried out to the gods of light, "Oh, help us, celestial ones! Someone has stolen Sagara's horse, and now his sons are creating havoc in their quest to find it. Mother Earth herself howls with pain!"

Finally, the sixty thousand and one sons came upon Lord Indra's sage, Kapila, deep in prayer. Nearby grazed the sacrificial horse. "Why, you horse thief!" yelled the sons in fury. But as they made to rush upon him to tear him limb from limb, Kapila turned and looked at them in such a blaze of fury that all sixty thousand and one sons were reduced to ashes.

King Sagara was heartbroken. Was there anyone who could save the souls of his sons and give them eternal life? What purification must he do? Sagara begged the gods for an answer.

"Only when the River Ganga flows to Earth and mingles with the ashes of your sons can they be purified and admitted into Heaven," said the gods.

So King Sagara returned to a life of prayer and austerity, doing everything he could to persuade the gods to allow the sacred river to flow to Earth. But he died with his sons' ashes still unpurified, leaving his descendants to continue his quest.

Thousands of years passed, and each descendant prayed as powerfully as the last, until the reign of King Bhagiratha. His devotions and penance were so saintlike that at last Lord Brahma agreed that the River Ganga should be released to fall to Earth. Finally, the souls of King Sagara's sixty thousand and one sons were to be redeemed.

The river gathered herself together, ready to unleash her waters, when Lord Shiva realized that such a torrent, if it fell

unhindered, could destroy the world. He threw himself beneath her mighty weight and spread out his hair across the heavens.

The River Ganga thundered forth, plunging into Shiva's locks and getting trapped and tangled up. So Shiva divided his hair into seven parts, and the waters flowed through it as seven tributaries, tumbling gloriously down from the sky with spray that scattered like white egrets. Everyone came out to watch: kings and warriors on their chariots; horses and elephants, their jewels flashing and sparkling like thousands of suns as they reflected the droplets of water; farmers in their fields; pilgrims and *rishis;* washerwomen and their children; Devas and demons. All the celestial beings came to gaze in awe at the silvery splendor streaming down through the sky, leaping with porpoises and turtles and flying fish arching like rainbows.

The river plunged down mountainsides, into canyons and valleys, filling brooks and streams, waterfalls and pools; it ran over rocks and down gulleys; and it rushed across the dry, thirsty plains of the Earth below.

King Bhagiratha leaped into his chariot and led the sacred Ganga's course to where the ashes of Sagara's sons lay. The river mingled with their ashes and, finally, released their souls. They rose, rejoicing, to eternal life in Heaven.

At last, King Sagara's wish was fulfilled. The people of Earth rejoiced; now everyone could bathe in the river and be purified.

How Ganesh Got His Elephant's Head

Lord Shiva was the god of Destruction—the Destroyer of Evil.

How fearsome he was, with snakes writhing in his hair, garlands of skulls from demons he had killed clattering around his neck, a tiger skin for a loincloth, and a trident in his hand. But most dangerous of all was Shiva's third eye. When closed, it was the inner eye of meditation: a link with the mind of God. But if he opened it, it was as deadly as an arrow.

His wife was Parvati, meaning Daughter of the Mountains, who spread peace and felicity wherever she went. But Parvati had moments of sadness. How often she sat alone in her mountain palace waiting for Lord Shiva to return.

She knew he was somewhere up in the snowy peaks, sitting in a yoga position, oblivious to the icy winds and numbing cold, deep in meditation. He was always praying.

Would he never stop? She longed to be with him, and most of all, she longed for a child.

How many times had she pleaded with him? "Oh, my husband, Lord Shiva, Blue-Throated and Three-Eyed, God of Gods, I do so wish for a child."

But Lord Shiva had only heaved a deep sigh, his mind already elsewhere, and left on another pilgrimage. Parvati had wept with frustration.

One day, she wandered onto the hillside. Fretfully, she played with the soft earth, molding it in her hands. As she pressed and squeezed, a small body began to take shape: a chubby torso, rounded limbs, and a firm head. Forgetting her sadness, Parvati delicately picked out tiny features in its face, and, suddenly, she found she had created the most beautiful baby boy.

How lovingly she gazed at his blank, expressionless face and stroked his stiff little body. "If only you were a real baby!" she murmured.

Her tears fell upon his face, and as they did, he smiled—a smile as radiant as a softly unfurling lotus flower, and he opened two round, glistening black eyes. From his lips came a miraculous word, "Mama!"

Parvati was overjoyed. "I have a baby!" she cried.

Unable to think of any single name that described how precious he was to her, she gave him one hundred names, including Heramba, Mother's Beloved Son; Avigna, Remover of Obstacles; Kriti, Lord of Music; and Akhuratha, One Who Has a Mouse as His Charioteer. But the one he was called by the most was Ganesh, Lord of the Throngs.

He grew quickly, and with such power and strength, he was soon his mother's fiercest protector.

Then one day, Lord Shiva returned. He hadn't heard about Ganesh, and Ganesh did not know what his father looked like. As Shiva entered the palace gates, Ganesh was horrified to see such a terrifying figure and ran forward to block his way. "Stop! How dare you enter my mother's palace?" he cried.

Shiva, furious at being challenged in his own home by such an impudent stripling, opened his third eye and cut off the boy's head.

Parvati's sorrow was dreadful. Her screams of horror echoed around the mountains.

"I'll put things right," soothed Shiva. "Ganesh shall have the head of the first living thing that is found facing north."

Messengers were sent all around the Universe. At last, one of them saw a mighty elephant whose head was turned northward. Not realizing it was Lord Indra's own elephant, which had come out of the Churning, the messenger struck off its head and triumphantly hurried back to Shiva, who immediately placed it on his son's shoulders.

Like the elephant, Ganesh now had wisdom, knowledge, and kindness. Parvati gave him another eight names, but the name she called him most of all was Gajanana, Elephant Face, and he became the most beloved of gods.

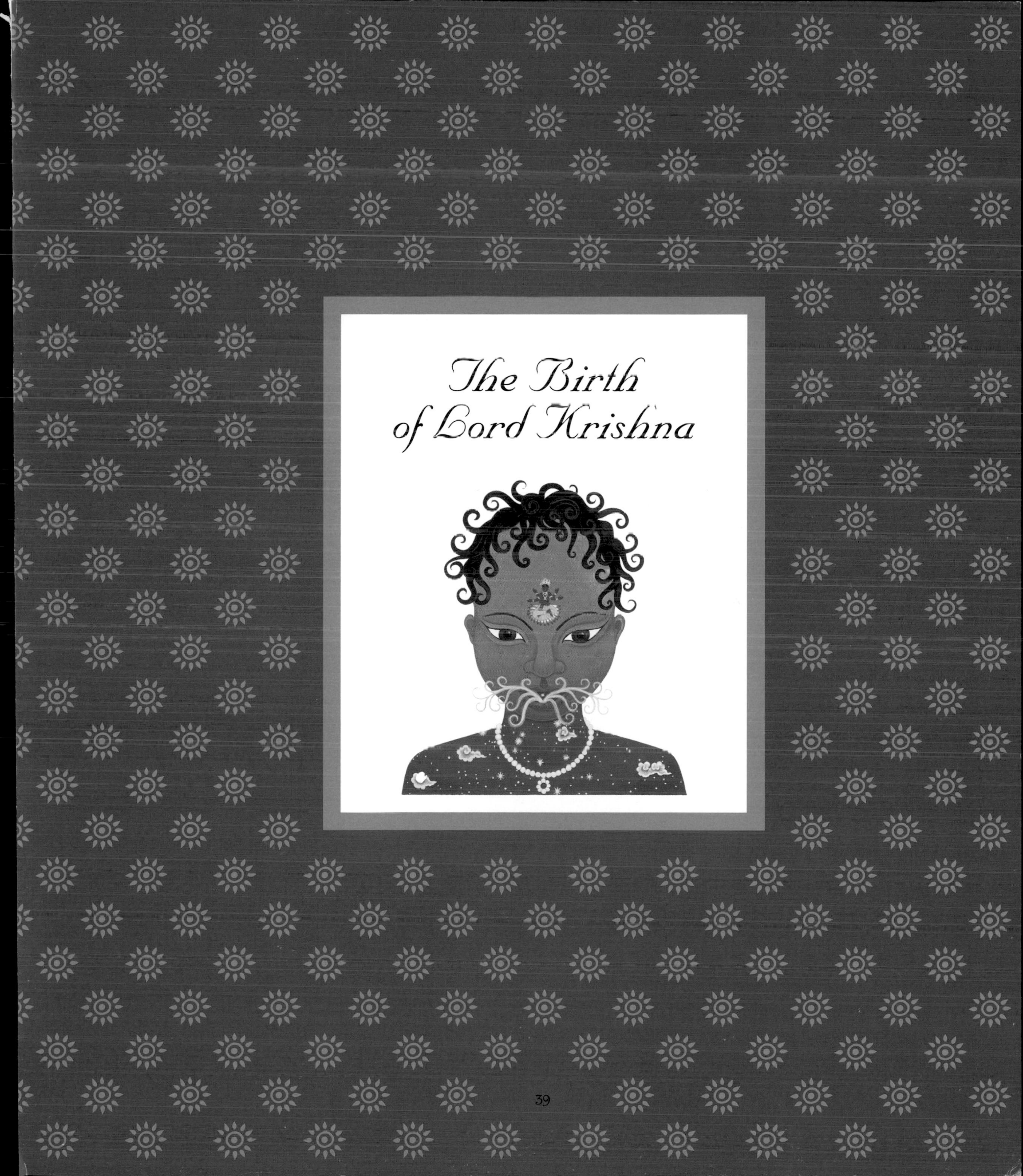

The Birth of Lord Krishna

Long ago, there was a wicked king called Kansa, who was told by his sages that one day he would be killed by the eighth child of his sister, Devaki.

Kansa was terrified and enraged. Devaki already had seven children, and it would be only a matter of time before she had an eighth child. Secretly, he plotted; on no account would he allow this child to be born. He devised a plan. He would put a guard on Devaki and her husband, Vasudeva, day and night, and the minute the child was born, he would have it destroyed. Kansa chose the most loyal of his

guards to carry out his orders, and made them promise utmost secrecy on pain of death. More than anything, he didn't want the gods to hear about his evil plan.

But the gods did hear about it, especially Lord Vishnu, the Preserver, the god of Goodness and Mercy.

Vishnu has the power to be an *avatar,* and be born again, taking on the form of any living thing. When he heard about Kansa's plan, Vishnu was filled with anger. He decided that not only would Devaki safely give birth to her eighth child, but he himself would be born as that child.

So Vishnu descended into the realm of the seeds of babies and made sure that it was he who was implanted in Devaki's womb. "She will give birth to me, and I will grow up to kill King Kansa," he vowed.

When Devaki was due to give birth, evil Kansa had her imprisoned with her husband in a windowless dungeon of stone. They were chained to the walls, and two guards sat on either side of the door. How Devaki wept at her brother's wickedness, and Vasudeva clenched his fists in anguish, wondering how he could save their baby.

When the moment arrived, it was the very middle of the night and a strange calm hung over the world. A full moon floated majestically over a still Earth. Not a creature moved; not a breath of wind stirred the leaves. Devaki and Vasudeva's

eighth child was born. As the dark, moist body of a baby boy slid into the world, a shiver of excitement vibrated around the Universe. Up in the heavens the drums thudded joyfully, and Lord Indra sent a shower of raindrops and flowers tumbling down from the sky.

The Devas and angels, *asparas* and *rishis* all burst into song. "Lord Vishnu is reborn as a man, and his name is Krishna!"

Devaki and Vasudeva waited fearfully. At any moment the child would cry, and King Kansa would know that a baby had been born.

Suddenly, Krishna opened his eyes. It was like the windows of Heaven opening. He gazed at his mother and father, and the chains fell from their bodies. He turned to the doors, and the locks flew open. Mysteriously, the guards were slumped in a deep sleep, and the women who had been brought in to help with the birth were snoring quietly in a corner.

"Quick! Escape! Save our baby!" cried Devaki.

Vasudeva gathered up the infant Krishna. "I'll take him somewhere safe," he whispered.

With tears of anguish, for she knew she would never see her baby again, Devaki kissed the little boy, murmuring her undying love, and then Vasudeva fled into the night.

Vasudeva hurried down to the river. He knew a cowherd called Nanda and his wife, Yasoda, who lived on the other

side. They were good, honest people who could be trusted implicitly. He would cross the river and ask Nanda and Yasoda to care for his son. But a terrible storm was brewing.

The winds blew violently; rain and hailstones slashed at Vasudeva's face, but still he stepped into the river. He fixed his eyes on the far bank while the waters swirled around him, rising

higher and higher. Soon they were up to his chest. Desperately, Vasudeva kept wading.

The waters kept on rising; soon they covered his shoulders and were lapping over his face. Just when he thought they must both drown, baby Krishna stretched out his foot and dipped a toe into the raging torrent. Immediately, the waters dropped, the wind and rain ceased, and Vasudeva was able to carry his son safely to the other side of the river.

In the dark of the night, Vasudeva handed his precious son to Nanda and Yasoda. When they looked upon the baby, they immediately loved him as their own child. "Don't worry, Vasudeva," they told him. "Krishna will be safe with us."

Bursting with sorrow, Vasudeva kissed his son farewell and waded back across the river.

So Krishna was brought up as the son of a cowherd. He seemed such a normal, happy boy, playing day in, day out with the village children. But he could be so naughty!

"Krishna, Krishna!" His name rang out across the fields. "Krishna is a naughty boy!" However, his name was never called in anger. No one could be cross with him for long; even though he liked hanging on to cows' tails and being dragged across the meadows; even though he teased the milkmaids and stole their milk and butter. He only had to flash his black eyes, or laugh and show his pearly white teeth, and all was forgiven.

Yasoda would watch her adopted son and feel a pang of fear, as all mothers do. She knew what dreadful dangers lurked for a naughty, active little boy. She feared the venomous serpent, which lay in wait by the river, and she feared the demon ogress who liked eating little children.

One day the village children rushed up to Yasoda, chanting, "Krishna is a naughty boy! Krishna is a naughty boy! He's being very bad!"

"What has he done now?" Yasoda sighed.

"He's eating chalk!" they proclaimed.

Yasoda ran over to her son and asked him, "Is it true? Have you been eating chalk?"

"No, I haven't," retorted Krishna. "The children are lying to get me into trouble."

"Open your mouth, then. Let me see," demanded Yasoda.

Krishna opened his mouth, and his mother looked inside. Time and space stood still.

Yasoda found herself gazing into the mouth of eternity; she saw Heaven and Earth and all the Cosmos; she saw mountains, rivers, jungles, and deserts. She even saw her own village, with the herdsmen in the fields. She saw the planets of the zodiac and the galaxies of the Universe; she saw earth, water, fire, and air; she gazed at eternity itself in the mouth of this boy who was Lord Vishnu born again.

When Krishna shut his mouth, Yasoda forgot everything she had seen, but she was left with a powerful understanding—she need never worry about him again. She didn't need to protect Krishna; he would protect her.

Her heart overflowing, Yasoda took the child onto her lap and was never afraid again.

Hanuman, the Greatest

Hanuman, the Monkey God, was son of the Wind God, Vayu.

He was the god of Air—the sustainer of all life. As well as being a musician, an actor, and a devout yogi, he had incredible powers. Hanuman could make himself as small as a mouthful of rice or as big as a mountain. He could fly through the air as swift as a thought, and he could make himself invisible.

He became Chief Minister to the King of the Monkeys, Sugriva, and everyone knew how wise Hanuman was.

One day, two strangers entered the kingdom of Sugriva. The monkeys chattered anxiously. Who were these men? Were they coming in peace, or with some dark purpose? Sugriva sent Hanuman to investigate and to bring them back to court if he was satisfied that they were friendly.

Hanuman soon came upon the men and for a while watched them secretly. Although these were two tall, strong, young warriors who carried their weapons boldly, the older one looked utterly grief-stricken and exhausted, while the younger was desperately trying to keep up his spirits. There was something noble about their faces—not only were they

handsome, but goodness shone from them as if they were gods. Hanuman stepped forward and made himself known.

"I am Hanuman, Chief Minister to Sugriva, King of the Monkeys. You have entered our kingdom, yet we do not know who you are. I have been instructed to invite you back to the palace, where we can offer you hospitality."

The two men were overjoyed at such kindness and gladly followed Hanuman through the forest.

"Who are you, and why do you enter my kingdom?" asked King Sugriva when they were brought before him.

The younger man spoke first. "Your Majesty, we are the sons of King Dasaratha of Ayodhya. My brother here is Prince Rama, the rightful ruler, and I am Lakshmana. Prince Rama was banished to the forest for fourteen years due to the jealousy of one of our father's wives, who wanted her son, Bharata, to be king when our good father felt too old to rule his kingdom. This is a death sentence, as the forest is full of wild animals and demons, so I insisted on accompanying my brother into exile. But alas, so too did his newly wedded wife, Princess Sita, because as a wife, she had sworn never to be parted from him. Now a great calamity has befallen us. Sita has disappeared, and we believe she has been kidnapped by demons."

"Alas, my lord, has anyone seen my beloved Sita?" exclaimed Prince Rama in a broken voice.

Deeply touched by their story, King Sugriva gave them fresh garments, food, and comfortable lodging, then sent word throughout his kingdom that if any monkey knew anything of the missing princess, he should immediately step forward.

One monkey did come forward, carrying a bracelet. "I was in the forest one day when this tumbled from the sky, and I glimpsed a flying chariot."

Lakshmana gave the bracelet to Prince Rama. "Brother! Do you recognize this? Is it Sita's?"

Rama tenderly held the bracelet in his fingers. "It could be," he stammered, his eyes blurred with tears. "I'm not sure."

"In which direction was the chariot flying?" asked King Sugriva.

"South," replied the monkey.

"Could it be that Princess Sita has been taken to the demon kingdom of Lanka?" asked Sugriva.

They shuddered to think that she had been kidnapped by Ravana, the King of the Demons.

"But how can we know for sure?" asked Lakshmana.

Hanuman bowed before Sugriva. "Sire! Let me go to Lanka. I can move in the skies without touching the Earth. I can toss the water out of the ocean up into the heavens and make the three worlds float. I will be quicker than lightning. If Princess Sita is there, I will find her."

"Take this ring," cried Rama, "so that she knows you come from me."

Then Hanuman leaped into the air and was away.

Fighting off ocean demons, he landed on the shores of Lanka and transformed himself into a cat. He searched the palace, but Sita was nowhere to be seen.

From the highest turret he looked in all directions. Suddenly in the far distance, he glimpsed a light. Turning back into a monkey, he leaped from tree to tree until at last, he found her.

She sat weeping beneath a bower, surrounded by evil demons who dozed and grunted in the moonlight. Hanuman wound his tail around a branch, hung upside down so that his mouth was near her ear, and whispered to her, "Noble princess, I come from Rama. Take heart. He is coming to rescue you!" And he gave her Rama's ring.

With a gasp of joy, she looked up, and he saw her ravaged face. Hanuman roared with rage. Spitting and screaming, the demons awoke and attacked.

Hanuman became gigantic. He tore up trees and killed hundreds of demons. But more and more swarmed all over him, and Hanuman was overwhelmed.

They dragged him before the King of the Demons.

Ravana was terrifying, with ten dreadful heads and twenty pitiless eyes—enough to chill even the bravest heart. "You thought you could rescue Sita, did you?" he sneered, while all around him the demons shrieked, "Kill, kill, kill!"

"No!" Ravana laughed. "Killing is too good for him. What is it a monkey values above all else?" The demons fell silent. "Why, his tail, of course! Set his tail on fire!"

The demons gleefully grasped blazing brands and set Hanuman's tail alight. Hanuman immediately shrank himself so small that he slipped out of their grasp and escaped. He sprang all over the demon city, setting it on fire with his burning tail, then returned triumphantly to the Monkey Kingdom.

Sita had been found! Hope surged through Rama's veins. With King Sugriva's help, he set about planning Sita's rescue. But how could they get an army across the ocean? There was only one way, and that was to build a bridge.

Everybody helped: armies of bears and monkeys ripped up trees, and even the ocean nymphs helped by throwing up vast boulders. Within five days, a bridge linked the mainland to the island of Lanka.

Rama and Sugriva's armies rushed across the bridge to be met by the demon army. There was a pitched battle. Prince Lakshmana fell, mortally wounded.

"My brother!" Rama cried brokenheartedly. "Who can save my brother?"

"I can!" exclaimed Hanuman, and in the blink of an eye, he sprang into the air and flew to the Himalayas. High up on a mountain grew an herb that had lifesaving qualities. Demons tried to block him, but Hanuman fought them off and made it to the icy slopes. He plucked the herb and, in just a few seconds, returned to rub the leaves into the dying prince's wounds.

He was alive! Lakshmana leaped to his feet and, alongside his brother, hurled himself back into battle.

Suddenly, there was King Ravana, with his ten heads and twenty blazing eyes. Rama fitted arrow after arrow, firing at each head, then striking it off with his sword. But as soon as one head fell, another rose in its place. In Rama's sheath of arrows was the golden arrow of Brahma—the only arrow that could defeat Ravana. But Rama knew he had only one try and must not fail. He fitted it to his bow, took aim at Ravana's heart, and fired.

The arrow struck home. With a horrible howl of disbelief, Ravana tottered, stumbled, and fell down dead.

Cheers echoed around the Universe. The demons fled or surrendered, and the two brothers stood, side by side, victorious.

Hanuman appeared, leading Sita through the chaos. The heavens sang as, joyfully, she fell at her husband's feet.

At last, Rama and Sita were together again and the exile was over. Gratefully, they thanked Sugriva and all the monkeys.

Hanuman pledged everlasting loyalty to Rama, and followed Rama, Sita, and Lakshmana back to the city of Ayodhya. They made their way through the forest, guided by oil lamps that had been placed there by devoted citizens who had waited so faithfully for their return. And temples were built in honor of the great, the most magnificent, the most loyal Monkey God, Hanuman.

The Choosing

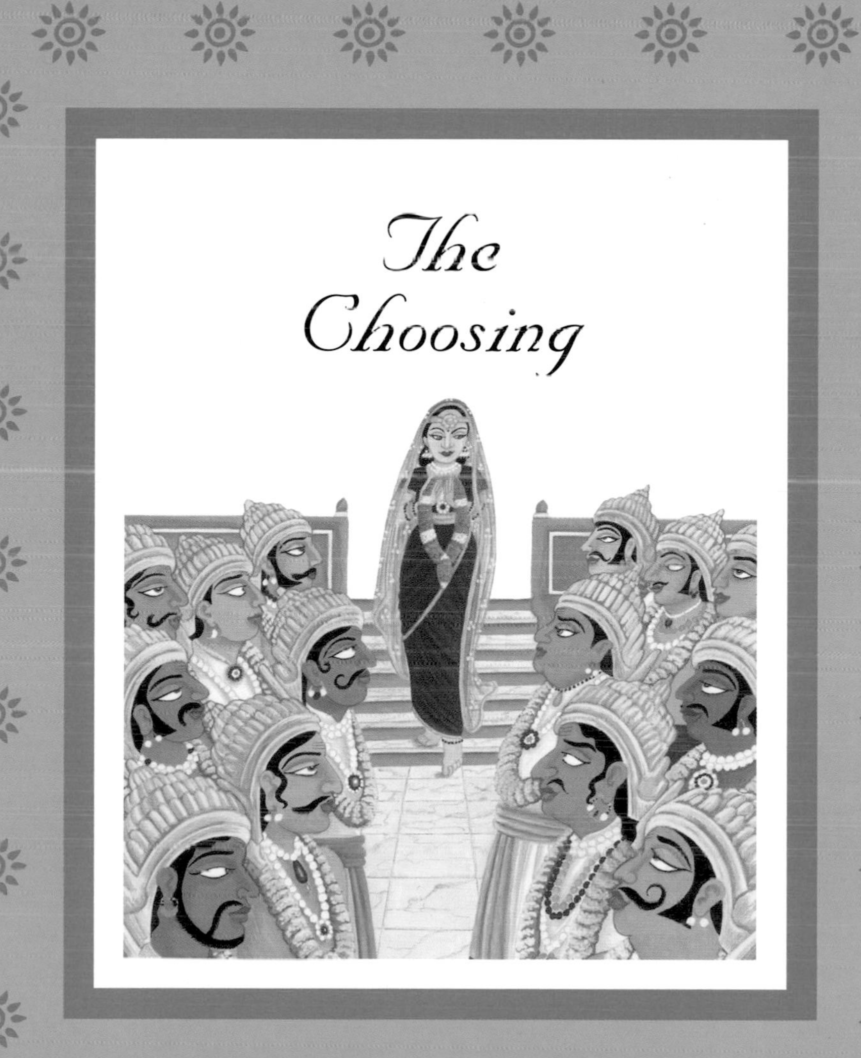

Everyone had heard of Damayanti,
the daughter of the king of Vidarbha.
Her beauty was so famous,
even the gods had heard of her.

King Nal, who was an incarnation of Manu, the first man on Earth, had of course heard about Damayanti's goodness and beauty, and he wondered if she might be the one to be his wife and queen.

The more Nal thought about her, the more he longed to see her, but he knew this would be difficult, as the custom was for the princess or her father to make the first move. He began spending long hours walking by the river, already deeply in love with a woman he had never met. If only he could get a message to her and tell her how much he loved her. But who could he trust with such a delicate mission?

He pined so much that one day he was approached by a swan, who came out of the river to ask why he was so sad and why he was neglecting his royal duties. When King Nal told the swan how badly he wanted to send a message to

Damayanti, the swan offered to be the messenger.

King Nal was overjoyed, and instantly agreed.

The swan flew to the palace gardens in Vidarbha and waited for the princess to take her daily walk by the river. Damayanti often liked to leave her chattering attendants and wander by herself, and it was then that the swan took the opportunity to approach her.

"Fair princess," he murmured, "I have come with a message from King Nal of Nishada. He wishes you to know that he loves you and wants you to be his queen." The swan then proceeded to describe this handsome, just, and good king. He spoke so movingly that the princess knew she returned King Nal's love. She told the swan she would inform her father that she was ready for marriage, and that her father would arrange

a *swayamvara* immediately. The *swayamvara,* or choosing ceremony, enabled a princess to summon all her suitors to stand before her so that she could place a garland around the neck of the man she chose to be her husband.

"Tell King Nal to come to my *swayamvara,*" she begged the swan, "and I will choose him."

The whole world was so excited on hearing the news that Damayanti was going to choose a husband, they stopped wars and campaigns and feverishly discussed whom she would favor.

Lord Indra, up in Heaven, began to wonder why no battle-slain warriors had come to him. "Ah," said a *rishi,* who had recently arrived. "It is because the Princess Damayanti is going to choose her husband."

Damayanti! At the sound of that name, other gods drew near—Agni, God of Fire; Varuna, Lord of the Waters; Yama, Lord of the Dead—they had all heard of Damayanti and her great beauty.

"Tell us more about this pearl among women," they begged the *rishi*.

"My lords, the people below can't think of anything else, and all the kings, princes, and warriors are galloping to attend her *swayamvara*."

"Then we must go, too," cried the gods, and leaped into their chariots.

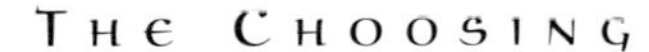

But even the gods needed someone to take a message to Damayanti, to tell her that she should choose one of them for a husband. If she did, it would mean she would become a goddess and no longer have to endure the travails of human life. But who would be their messenger?

Looking down from their chariots, they noticed a very handsome king, shining with joy and goodness. They were sure they could trust him.

They floated down through the blue air and landed before an astonished King Nal.

"Who are you?" he stammered, falling to his knees.

"We are Indra, Agni, Varuna, and Yama, the Guardians of the Earth. We wish you to present our petition before the princess and request that she choose one of us for her husband."

Nal went pale. "I beg you, my lords, please don't send me on this mission. I, too, love Damayanti, so how can I be the one to plead your case?"

But the gods were adamant. "Go!" they ordered, and in a twinkling, King Nal found himself before her.

Everything he had heard was true—she was more beautiful than the Moon, and her startled eyes were like dark pools of magic.

When Damayanti saw this glorious man standing before her, she could hardly breathe. "Who are you?" she whispered.

"I am Nal," he replied with a breaking heart. "I bring a message from the Four Guardians of the Earth. You are to choose one of them for your husband."

Damayanti's eyes filled with tears. "I have already made my choice," she stammered. "You are the one I want, and now that I have seen you, I know how much I love you."

"We cannot disobey the gods," said Nal sadly.

Suddenly, Damayanti brushed away her tears and stood taller. "Take this message back to the gods. Tell them to attend my *swayamvara,* but promise me, O king, that you will come too. It is you I will choose, and the gods know that even they will have to accept my choice."

Full of despair, Nal returned to the Guardians of the Earth and gave them her message. But he feared for her. No one could disobey the gods.

The day of the *swayamvara* arrived. What a mighty throng of *rajahs* and princes assembled to await the princess; all were fiercely shining, decked in jewels and as magnificent as tigers. Some were proud, some battle-scarred, some as smooth as serpents. All were festooned with flowers.

The princess emerged, carrying her garland. Her eyes scanned the expectant faces. But there was only one face she was looking for.

Joyfully, she saw it. She raised her garland, ready to drop

it around Nal's neck, when suddenly she faltered. Instead of one King Nal standing before her, there were five—all perfectly identical, and all looking at her with eyes brimming with love. The gods had tricked her!

Damayanti clasped her hands in prayer. "O my lords! Understand that I love King Nal and have vowed that he will be my husband. A vow is holy. I beg you to help me keep it. Show me the true Nal!"

No one moved. The midday sun burned down on the palace. The shadows of the suitors were etched sharp among the pillars. In their flowing robes and jewels, the *rajahs* and warriors began to perspire, the flowers around their necks wilted, and their garments became dusty. But Damayanti noticed that four of the five Nals stayed dry, fresh, and perfect.

She stared at them. Four Nals stared back at her, unblinking. Gods never blink, but the fifth Nal blinked against the sun. Four had skin as dry as baked clay, but the face of the fifth Nal trickled with moisture. The flowers around the necks of four of them stayed fresh, but everyone else's wilted in the heat. Across the floor, the shadows of the waiting princes deepened to purple, but four of the Nals cast no shadows. Damayanti's heart was filled with hope. Her eyes lowered slowly. Four pairs of feet hovered just a little off the ground, but the fifth Nal stood firmly on the marble floor.

"I choose you," cried Damayanti joyfully, flinging her garland around the neck of the fifth and true Nal.

So Nal and Damayanti were married. The four gods gave their blessings, for they knew that once a vow had been made, that vow was sacred and could never be broken.

The Battle of Eighteen Days

In the dead of night,
a young princess secretly crept down
to the river, carrying her newborn
son in a basket.

Who would believe that his father was Surya, the Sun God? She would be disgraced. Weeping, she lowered the basket into the fast-running waters, to be carried wherever the river took it, and prayed that the gods would care for her baby.

The little boy was found by a simple charioteer and his wife who, being childless, thought this was an answer to their prayers. They brought him up as their own son.

Later, the young princess, whose name was Kunti, married King Pandu. Pandu had been made ruler because his older brother, Dhritarashtra, was blind. Though Dhritarashtra later had a hundred sons known as the Kauravas, King Pandu was cursed and unable to have children. However, the gods enabled Kunti to give birth to five sons. Just as Kunti's secret firstborn had been fathered by a god, so too were her other five sons fathered by gods, and they became known as the Pandavas.

Even as young children, the Pandavas and Kauravas were rivals, always trying to outdo each other in archery, sword fighting, and hunting. As they grew to manhood, they competed even more fiercely, for not only were the Kauravas full of jealousy because the Pandavas always outshone them, but they seethed with resentment, believing that their blind father had been deeply wronged and should still be king.

One day, there was a royal tournament in which everyone in the land had been invited to compete. Once again, the Pandavas demonstrated their brilliance, and once again they outshone their cousins the Kauravas with their skills and bravery.

The tournament was nearly over; the Pandavas were about to leave the field with their prizes and trophies, when a stranger appeared. Clad in golden armor and clattering with weapons, the stranger marched up to Arjuna, the finest man among the Pandava brothers, and challenged him, crying out, "I can match

any skill that you have, and better. Let me prove it to you. Fight me hand to hand in equal combat!"

Murmurs of astonishment ran through the crowds. Who was this mysterious warrior with the impudence to challenge

Prince Arjuna? Yet the warrior shone with golden light and had an air of nobility. Arjuna turned to him in annoyance. "Do you not know that a prince may only compete with a warrior of equal rank?" His voice was full of scorn. "What are you? Begone!"

But the Kauravas, sensing that this stranger might equal Arjuna in combat, taunted their cousin. "Are you afraid to accept the challenge?" they jeered. "Come on. Let the warrior prove his worth!"

At that moment, an old charioteer ran out from the crowds and clasped the stranger. "Karna! My son! Where have you been? I've been looking for you everywhere!"

Everybody burst out laughing. A lowborn charioteer's son had dared to challenge Prince Arjuna. He must be mad!

Prince Arjuna was about to stride away, feeling vindicated, when the leader of the Kauravas, Duryodhana, shouted, "Wait! If it is simply rank that is standing in the way of a challenge, then I give part of my kingdom to Karna!" He embraced the charioteer's son. "From henceforth, you shall be known as King Karna of Anga!"

The crowd seethed with excitement. Arjuna was furious. He felt tricked, but realized he had no option but to take up the challenge. He walked into the center of the arena, and Karna took up an opposing position.

At that moment, Queen Kunti, who had been watching, looked into the golden face of Karna and realized he was her firstborn son. Stricken with grief that two of her sons were about to fight to the death, she fainted away.

In sympathy, it seemed, the Sun dipped behind a black cloud and the sky darkened to night. It was time to pray and make offerings to the gods, so the fight was postponed and people made their way home, some saying Arjuna was clearly the better, but others saying Karna would be the victor.

Because the Kauravas had supported him, Karna pledged everlasting loyalty to them and their cause to destroy the Pandavas. But the gods were perturbed, and Lord Krishna, alarmed that Karna was unaware of his birthright, came to him in secret and told him the truth of his birth. "Kunti is your mother and the Pandavas your true brothers. Now that you know the truth, do not continue with this deadly fight. Make peace with them, and they will honor you as their true elder."

But Karna was bitter. "Why should I love a mother who gave me up, and why should I not hate Arjuna and the Pandavas for seeking to humiliate me? No! I pledged my loyalty to the Kauravas, and a pledge can never be broken."

"Then know this, Karna," said Krishna sadly. "I am pledged to support the Pandavas, and when you meet in battle, I shall be Arjuna's charioteer."

What greater enmity can there be than that of brother against brother? After many dreadful conflicts and bloodshed, the Pandavas, led by Arjuna, and the Kauravas, led by Karna, prepared for a final battle. They gathered on a vast plain that glinted with clashing shields and spears and fluttered with flags from end to end.

The night before the battle, Arjuna asked Lord Krishna to drive him down to a place between the opposing armies.

Gathering the reins of his five white horses as if harnessing his five senses, Krishna drove them down to the plain. In the stillness, Arjuna gazed at the thousands of sleeping warriors, recognizing every one—for were they not all his own flesh and blood: cousins, fathers, brothers, sons, and uncles? He dropped his warrior's bow and fell back weeping. "Ah, Krishna! I have no stomach for this war. I seek no victory. Oh, day of darkness, how have we come to this, that we are about to fight our own kith and kin?"

But Krishna said, "What you see is not the truth. You do not fight mortals, but evil. This is a battle that must be won. Death is just throwing off an old garment for a new one—an old life for a new. Trust in me, Arjuna, for I am the Light."

So began the Battle of Eighteen Days. At each pale dawn, the warriors faced each other, and at each red sunset, the battlefield ran with blood.

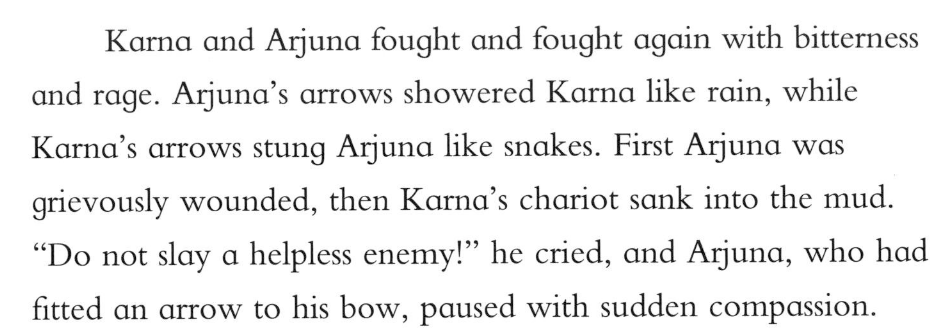

Karna and Arjuna fought and fought again with bitterness and rage. Arjuna's arrows showered Karna like rain, while Karna's arrows stung Arjuna like snakes. First Arjuna was grievously wounded, then Karna's chariot sank into the mud. "Do not slay a helpless enemy!" he cried, and Arjuna, who had fitted an arrow to his bow, paused with sudden compassion.

But Krishna intervened: "O Arjuna! Remember the misdeeds of the Kauravas! Remember how you were helpless when your bow broke, but Karna still fired arrows at you. Remember how he mercilessly killed your son."

Arjuna let fly his arrow, and Karna fell dead.

At last the Pandavas had defeated the Kauravas. Evil was overcome and the gods triumphant.

But the Pandavas were unable to rejoice in their victory after such slaughter. Casting off their royal garments, they set off on a long and arduous pilgrimage to the sacred mountain of Meru. One by one, they died of exhaustion on the way, only to find themselves reunited at the gates of Heaven, where they were welcomed by Lord Indra and Lord Krishna. Waiting to greet them were their cousins the Kauravas, shining in new garments of life. Now they could forget their quarrels and embrace each other as brothers.

Full of joy, Arjuna and Karna entered the Celestial City side by side.

Three Steps to Save the Universe

Since time began and until time ends, there will always be wars between the Devas and the Asuras, the gods and the demons.

Bali was descended from the great demon king Hiranyakshipu, who had fought many battles with the gods, especially Lord Vishnu, who had defeated him.

But when Bali became king, he decided on a different tactic. Instead of going to war with the gods, he would behave in a saintlike way: do good, rule well, and make the people love him so much that it would weaken the power of the gods.

So he stopped his demons from being destructive and became very pious. He lived simply, with great austerity, often undertaking extreme acts of penance, for which he became admired and trusted. The people of Earth loved him dearly. They saw him as benevolent, generous, and just, and welcomed him as their ruler.

So Bali now ruled not only the Underworld, but Earth, too, and the third world, Heaven, would be next.

The gods began to worry. Bali seemed unstoppable. When their worst fears were realized and he ousted Indra, Lord of

Heaven, the gods went to Lord Vishnu, the Divine Preserver, and begged him to recognize the danger.

"Bali is the greatest threat to the Cosmos. He is now ruler of all three worlds. If he is not stopped, the demons will conquer the Universe and the power of the gods will be destroyed."

Lord Vishnu listened gravely and decided he must become an *avatar* and be born again as a human. In due course, he took on the form of a dwarf called Vamana.

At first glance he seemed insignificant, this deformed,

black-skinned man, looking like a poor pilgrim with his water pot under one arm and a stick in the other, his body covered by a single saffron cloth held by a lion skin.

People were scornful when they heard that Vamana was going to court to beg the king's charity. What a presumption!

But King Bali, whose reputation was as a benevolent ruler, invited Vamana to come before him, even though one of his own demon advisers warned against it. "Sire, this could be a trick of the gods. There is something about this dwarf Vamana that disturbs me. He could be in disguise. Beware!"

But King Bali had now become so powerful, so sure of himself, that he was deaf to anything else except his own ambitions. Not only did he feel invulnerable and invincible, but in his arrogance, he wanted to demonstrate his supreme benevolence before this pitiful *Brahman*.

"What is it you want, O pious pilgrim, son of a Brahman? Tell me, and you have my word it shall be yours. A cow of pure gold, perhaps? A beautiful palace for your comfort, prosperous villages, horses, and elephants? Or perhaps the beautiful daughter of a Brahman?" Bali took up a vessel of purified water to clinch his promise. "Tell me your wish and you have my word, it shall be yours."

The small, deformed, black-skinned man bowed submissively before him.

"Sire," stammered the dwarf, "all I ask is for a piece of land that I can cross with three steps."

King Bali roared with laughter. Three steps from this little man would barely be enough room to fit a bed.

Again, his demon adviser warned the king. "Do not grant this request, my lord," he begged. "Better to break your promise than risk losing everything you own."

But King Bali felt he would lose face if he denied such a modest demand, so he cried, "Vamana! You shall have your wish. Three steps of land."

At this moment, the little dwarf began to grow. He grew and grew, taller than the trees and the mountains, broader than the oceans, so huge that he blotted out the skies above. He took his first step and claimed the whole Earth; he took his second step and claimed back Heaven. He was about to take his third step and claim the Underworld when King Bali flung himself to the ground in sorrow and surrender. "Don't make your third step!" he pleaded, and in an act of humility, he placed his head on the ground. "Mighty Lord Vishnu! I beg of you—crush me instead."

Vishnu placed his foot on top of Bali's head. A great wail of sorrow rang throughout the land. His people were grief-stricken at the thought that they would never see their beloved king again.

"Return to the Underworld, where you belong," thundered

Vishnu. "But because you have done good and the people love you, you shall return to Earth for one day in every year." Then he pressed his foot on Bali's head and pushed him down through the earth, back into the Kingdom of the Demons.

The Author

Jamila Gavin was born in the foothills of the Himalayas in Mussoorie, India. With an Indian father and an English mother, Jamila has always considered herself lucky to belong to two countries and to have inherited two different cultures. Even her name, Jamila (Arabic) Elizabeth (Jewish/Christian) Khushal-Singh (Hindu/Sikh), reflects her multicultural background.

At school in India and then in England, where her family settled, Jamila excelled at music and English. However, she secretly preferred gymnastics, and was so good at walking on her hands that she daydreamed about running away to become a circus acrobat.

Instead, Jamila studied music in London, Paris, and Berlin before joining the BBC to work on music and arts programs. Jamila was married with two children by the time her first book was published in 1979. She is now a highly respected author and admits that, although she can no longer walk on her hands, she can still stand on her head.

The Artist

Amanda Hall first fell in love with India while visiting Rajasthan and the city of Udaipur, famous for painters who create intricately detailed miniatures featuring beautiful, jewel-like images of elephants, rajahs, *and palaces. To her, the city "seemed to glitter in a white haze of sunlight."*

Inspired by cultures from across the globe, Amanda enjoys immersing herself in a country's visual traditions before she begins illustrating. During her research for Tales from India, *she found Indian miniature paintings from the eighteenth century to be particularly intriguing. She went on to combine elements of these with her own style.*

Although she usually works in watercolor, crayon, or ink, Amanda used gouache for this artwork, as it is traditionally used in Indian miniatures and is ideal for creating vibrant colors. Amanda imagines that the Udaipur painters must have excellent eyesight—in order to capture the fine detail in this book, she had to paint looking through a gigantic magnifying glass, which she wore around her neck, and the smallest brush she used had only one or two hairs.

Glossary

avatar A god who has taken on a human or animal form to come to Earth.

aspara A nymph. A friend to the Devas.

Brahman A member of the highest of the four main Hindu castes, or social divisions. The priestly caste.

egret A long-legged water bird with white plumage; found across India.

garland A necklace of threaded flowers.

kith and kin Friends and relatives.

pilgrim A person journeying to a sacred place for religious reasons.

rajah An Indian king or prince.

rishi A demigod, born from the mind of Lord Brahma.

swayamvara An ancient ceremony in which a princess chooses a husband.

yogi A person who is highly skilled at yoga, the spiritual practice of mind and body.